I AM HELPING

BY MERCER MAYER

Random House 🏠 New York

Copyright © 1992 by Mercer Mayer. Little Critter® is a registered trademark of Mercer Mayer.
All rights reserved under International and Pan-American Copyright Conventions. Originally published
in a different format by B. Dalton Booksellers, Inc., a division of Barnes and Noble Bookstores, Inc.
This edition published in the United States by Random House, Inc., New York, and simultaneously
in Canada by Random House of Canada Limited, Toronto.
Library of Congress Catalog Card Number: 94-68287   ISBN 0-679-87348-1
Manufactured in Italy   10 9 8 7 6 5 4 3 2 1

🐸 GREEN FROG PUBLISHERS, INC. / J. R. SANSEVERE BOOK

I am a good helper.

I help wash the clothes.
I help get them dirty, too.

I help sweep the porch.

I help cut the grass.

I help make the beds.

I help take out the trash.

I help with the shopping.

I help feed the baby.

I help burp him, too.

I help fix the window.

I help dust the furniture.

I help vacuum the rug.

I help pick apples.

I help weed the garden.

I help watch the baby.

I help make a pie.

I help eat the pie, too.

Mom and Dad sure are lucky
that I am such a good helper.